Bath time for John

For Max

Library of Congress Catalog Card No. 88–80588

ISBN 0–316–32304–7
10 9 8 7 6 5 4 3 2 1

First published in Great Britain in 1985
by Hamish Hamilton Children's Books

Printed in Hong Kong by
South China Printing Co.

Bath time for
John

Bob Graham

Little, Brown and Company
Boston   Toronto

It's bath time for John.

It's a wet time for Theo,

and a wet time for Sarah.

Sarah keeps watch.

John can't be left by himself.

He is too young.

John has a wind-up frog.

Sarah winds it up and off it goes.

It bangs into the side

and just keeps swimming.

Theo drinks John's bath water

and picks up the green frog.

Off he goes,

leaving a trail of water.

John climbs slowly out of the bath.

Sarah is right behind Theo.

John is skidding . . .

. . . and crawling.

Sarah is wild.

Theo is racing. Look at him go!

"DROP IT, THEODORE."

Theo has nowhere to go.

John has caught up.

He has leaves and dirt sticking to him.

"YOU BAD DOG, THEODORE."

There are tooth marks on the plastic frog.

John gets back into his cold grey bath.

There is one leg missing.

Now the frog goes round and round.